W9-DAG-472

A ZOO FOR MISTER MUSTER

Arnold Lobel

HarperCollins Publishers

for Anita, Adrianne and Adam

A ZOO FOR MISTER MUSTER
Copyright © 1962 by Arnold Lobel
Copyright renewed 1990 by Adam Lobel
All rights reserved. No part of this book may be used or
reproduced in any manner whatsoever without written
permission except in the case of brief quotations embodied in
critical articles and reviews. Printed in Mexico. For information
address HarperCollins Children's Books, a division of
HarperCollins Publishers, 10 East 53rd Street, New York,
NY 10022.

Library of Congress Catalog Card Number: 62-7313
ISBN 0-06-023990-5
ISBN 0-06-023991-3 (lib. bdg.)

A ZOO FOR MISTER MUSTER

Every sunny day Mister Muster
put on his vest and coat and hat

and walked happily along the street to his favorite place ... the park zoo.

Mister Muster loved all the
animals in the zoo and
all the animals in the zoo
loved Mister Muster.
The elephants trumpeted loudly
when they saw him coming
through the entrance gate.

The lions began to roar. The birds and monkeys screeched and chattered their welcome.

There was so much noise that the zookeeper
had to put his fingers in his ears.

Mister Muster always spent the whole day at the zoo.

When night came Mister Muster felt sad.
He hated to say good-bye to the animals
and they hated to say good-bye to him.
"I only live at the end of the street,"
sighed Mister Muster. "But it seems far, far away
when I must leave my friends."

Mister Muster did not live alone.
He had two goldfish in a large bowl
and a canary that sang all the time.
Still, when it was rainy or snowy or
sleety and Mister Muster
could not go to the zoo,
he felt lonely and missed
his friends very much.

One day, while the zookeeper was taking a nap,
an elephant took away his key.

That night the elephant opened all the cage doors. The animals knew exactly what they wanted to do.

They walked to the big apartment house where Mister Muster lived and tiptoed past the doorman.

Mister Muster had just gone to bed
when his doorbell rang.

"Goodness gracious," said
Mister Muster when he found
all of his friends outside
the door. "Come in, oh do
come in!" he said.

The next morning the zookeeper
could not believe his eyes.
"My animals are gone, they're
gone!" he cried.
The policemen came and began
searching everywhere.

In the apartment house where Mister Muster lived
someone saw an elephant in the elevator and a
hippopotamus in the hallway. Some strange things
began to happen and some strange noises were heard
from behind Mister Muster's door.

Someone called the police and they came quickly.
The zookeeper came with them.
The policemen knocked loudly on Mister Muster's door.
"Open up in the name of the law," they cried.

The door opened slowly.
There stood Mister Muster.
"Good day, gentlemen, won't you
join us for lunch," he said.

In the middle of the table
was a huge chocolate cake
that Mister Muster had baked.

The zookeeper and the policemen
were too surprised to speak.
Finally the zookeeper said,
"All these animals must come back
to the zoo at once!"
At this, there was a great roaring
and trumpeting and screeching as the animals
ran from the table to find hiding places.
"Halt in the name of the law,"
shouted the policemen.

The animals hid in the bathroom,

and in the bedroom...
any place they could find.

"Mister Muster," said the zookeeper,
"perhaps they will listen to you.
Please, please Mister Muster, ask them
to come back to the zoo. If you can
do this, I'll do anything for you...
I'll make you an assistant zookeeper
with a uniform and a badge."

When they heard this,
all the animals jumped from
their hiding places. They all marched back
to the zoo with Mister Muster in the lead.

Soon the animals were happily in their cages
at the park zoo. And happiest of all was Mister Muster,
with his uniform, his badge and all of his friends
close by all the time.

M. MUSTER
ASSISTANT
ZOOKEEPER
ON DUTY
24 HOURS A DAY